MONKEY BUSINESS

EX LIBRIS

· SHIRLEY CLIMO ·

MONKEY BUSINESS

STORIES FROM AROUND THE WORLD

ILLUSTRATED BY
ERIK BROOKS

Henry Holt and Company
New York

Henry Holt and Company, LLC
Publishers since 1866
115 West 18th Street
New York, New York 10011
www.henryholt.com

Henry Holt is a registered trademark of Henry Holt and Company, LLC
Text copyright © 2005 by Shirley Climo
Illustrations copyright © 2005 by Erik Brooks
All rights reserved.
Distributed in Canada by H. B. Fenn and Company Ltd.

Library of Congress Cataloging-in-Publication Data
Climo, Shirley.
Monkey business: stories from around the world / Shirley Climo; illustrated by Erik Brooks.
p. cm.
ISBN-13: 978-0-8050-6392-9
ISBN-10: 0-8050-6392-7
1. Monkeys—Juvenile literature. 2. Monkeys—Folklore—Juvenile literature.
I. Brooks, Erik, ill. II. Title.
QL737.P9 C53 2004   599.8 22   2003063956

First Edition—2005
Designed by Amy Manzo Toth
Manufactured in China
1 3 5 7 9 10 8 6 4 2

The artist used colored pencil and watercolor on paper to create the illustrations for this book.

To Nina, who kept faith with the monkeys—
and with me
—S. C.

For my adventurous brothers
Ryan and Colby—crazy monkeys!
—E. B.

AUTHOR'S NOTE

◆ ◆ ◆ ◆ ◆ ◆ ◆ ◆ ◆ ◆ ◆ ◆ ◆ ◆ ◆ ◆ ◆ ◆ ◆

My own monkey business began with a folktale from Africa, "The People of the Trees." Before I could retell this lively story from the Congo, I needed to learn about the people who'd once lived there and about the monkeys who had shared the rain forest with them. My research led me to a variety of monkey lore. I carried home pounds of volumes from my local library, haunted used bookstores for out-of-print treasures, and searched for current primate material online. Eventually, my collection included monkey tales from the Americas and Asia as well as from Africa, and I'd added some fables and proverbs to the mix.

For each story, I suggested a likely species of monkey. Monkeys vary widely in appearance, intelligence, and behavior, so matching monkey to manuscript was a challenge. It has kept me as busy as a monkey in a peanut patch for quite some time, but I've had a lot of fun.

Contents

◆ ◆

Introduction

❖ ❖

Wherever in the world we live, we belong to one species. We're human beings.

Our closest relatives in the animal kingdom are apes and monkeys. There are only five types of apes: gorillas, chimpanzees, and bonobos in Africa, and orangutans and gibbons in Asia. But look at the monkeys! There are more than a hundred different species of them.

At one time, monkeys were spread over much of the earth, but now there are fewer monkeys in fewer places. With the coming of the last ice age, they disappeared from all but the warmer regions. Of the six inhabited continents, only Australia never was home to monkeys. Separated for millions of years from the rest of the world, that continent developed its own unique animals.

Today about half of the monkeys live in Central and South America. They're called New World monkeys. All of them are tree dwellers, and many have prehensile, or grasping, tails for holding on.

The other half, the Old World monkeys, are in Africa and Asia. Some live in trees, some on the ground, but none can hold on with their tails. Most have thumbs for grasping.

In this book are monkey stories, monkey facts, and monkey sayings. Find out for yourself what the world's monkey business is about!

Monkeys in Africa and Madagascar

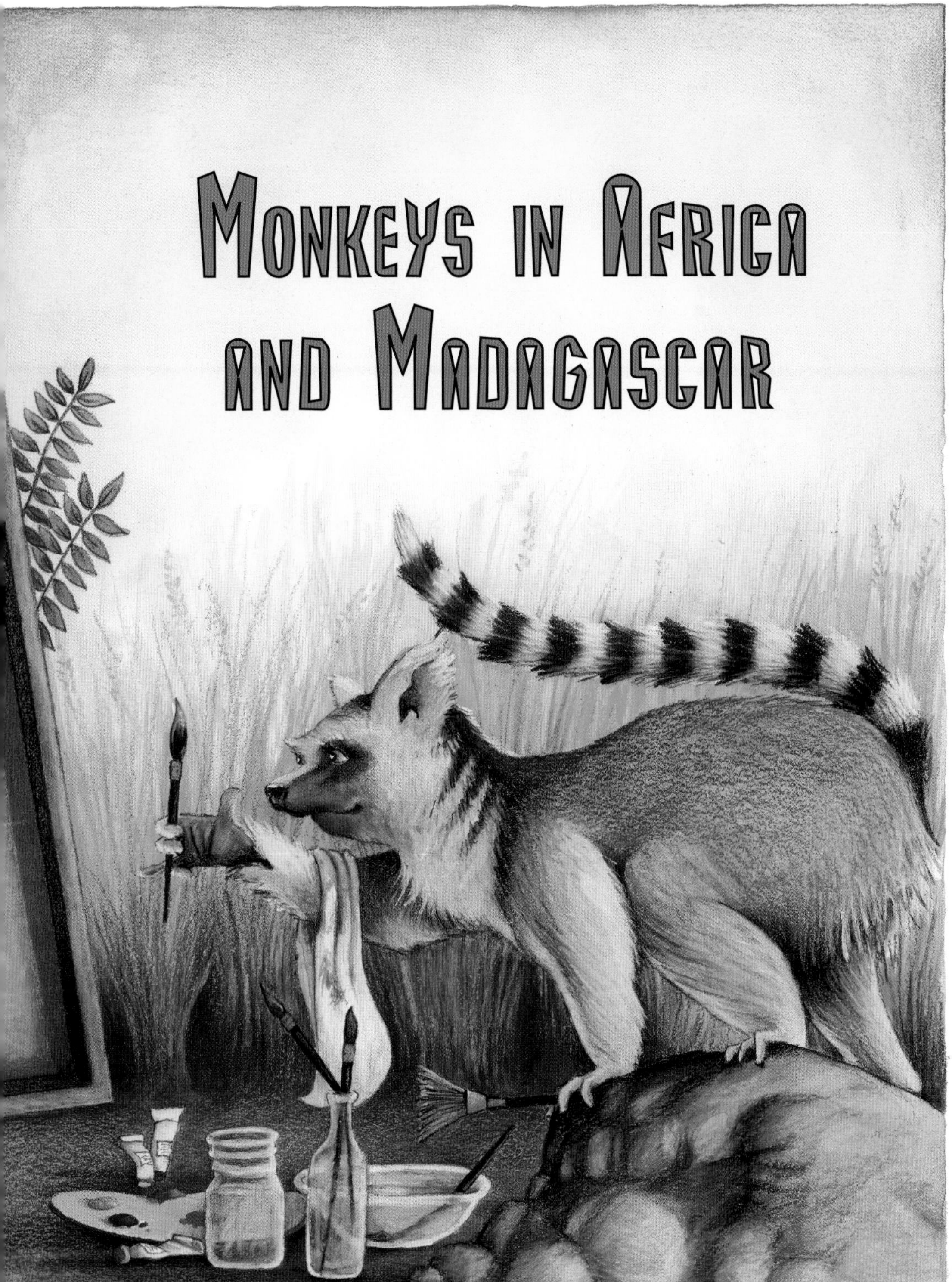

Why a Monkey's Not a Man

◆ A WEST AFRICAN FABLE ◆

*Story tellers everywhere have offered explanations for the
antics of the animals that share their land and their lives.
This how-it-happened monkey fable comes from the
Republic of Benin. Benin still has varied animal life,
including antelope, wild pigs, elephants, panthers,
lions—and monkeys.*

When Mahu the Mother Goddess was making the world, she
fashioned people first. She dug clay from the earth, rolled it
between her palms until it was smooth, and shaped it into
men and women and children.

After she completed the people, she began to make the
birds that fly in the air, the beasts that walk on the land, and
all the fish that swim in the rivers and the sea. There were
so many creatures to make, large and small, that she grew
weary. So she asked some animals that she had already
finished—the hippopotamus, the lion, and the monkey—for
their help.

"I gave you five fingers on each hand," Mahu said to the
monkey, "so you should do especially well. If you work

hard, I shall place you with the people and not among the animals."

The monkey got hold of his tail and turned a somersault. Then he sprang through the forest, jumping from tree to tree, squawking to those below, "Look at me! I am a people-animal!"

The next morning, Mother Mahu came to see what the beasts had accomplished. The hippo had dug up a huge pile of wet clay. The lion had patted it smooth with his paw. But the monkey had spent all day showing off and bragging, "I am going to be a man!"

"No." The goddess shook her head. *"One who wastes time boasting will always be a monkey."*

The People of the Trees

• A STORY FROM THE CONGO •

The small people in the story are the Efe, called Pygmies by outsiders. For hundreds of years, the Efe used seashells as trading money.

The leaf-eating monkeys who live high in the tropical rain forest canopy are the black-and-white colobus. These shy monkeys are known in the Congo as the People of the Trees.

Long ago, before leopards had spots or goats grew beards, an old man and his wife lived in a little village at the edge of the great green jungle.

All the huts in the village were shaped like anthills and thatched with mongongo leaves to keep out the rain. Each hut had a hole in the roof to let smoke go out and a larger hole in the side to let people come in.

All the villagers were small in size, but the old man and his wife were by far the smallest. He was as skinny as one of his own arrows. She was as scrawny as the neck bone of a chicken. When a breeze blew, they had to wrap their arms about each other to keep from tipping over.

What the two old people lacked in size, they made up for

in wits. They loved to play jokes on each other or on anyone else in the village. No others were as clever when it came to getting what they wanted. Something always disappeared if the skinny old man or scrawny old woman was about.

"They are much too old for such mischief," the neighbors grumbled.

One morning, the skinny old man and the scrawny old woman decided to visit the village headman, for he had hurt his toe. When they ducked through the door hole of his hut, they found him sitting on his mat, counting a pile of shiny *jimbu* shells.

In the dim light, these shells from the sea glistened like stars in the sky. The skinny old man had never seen such treasure. "How lucky you are!" he told the headman.

The scrawny old woman longed to hold a shell. But what she said to the headman was "How unlucky you are to have a sore toe. Can you stand up?"

The headman dropped the *jimbu* shells into a sack without a word.

"If you cannot stand up, then you cannot walk," the old man suggested.

"If you cannot walk, then you cannot run," his wife added.

The skinny old man grinned at the scrawny old woman. "And you cannot chase us either!" he cried. Snatching the bag of shells, the two dashed from the hut.

The astonished headman could not stand or walk or run, but he could make noise. He blew an ear-aching screech on his bone whistle.

Alarmed, the villagers came running. When they heard

what had happened, their alarm turned to anger. Now the old couple had gone too far. The *jimbu* shells belonged to everyone in the village. All of them—except the headman—ran after the old man and the old woman.

"Can't catch us!" crowed the skinny old man. He fled into the forest with the old woman just a footstep behind.

The farther they ran, the closer the villagers got. The faster they hurried, the heavier the sack of shells became. At last the skinny old man and the scrawny old woman came to a tree so tall that clouds caught in its topmost limbs.

Panting, the husband pointed to the tree. "Could we?" he asked.

Breathless, the wife nodded.

The two scrambled up the tree, squeezing past a python twisted about the trunk and scattering a swarm of blue

butterflies. They did not rest until they reached the high branches where the bee-eater bird roosted.

Moments later, the angry villagers arrived. "Give us back our *jimbus*!" they shouted.

The two in the tree chuckled. This was their best joke yet. They shook the bag of shells. "Come up and get them!"

Those beneath the tree scowled. Even the smallest of the village elders was too heavy for the slender branches. Even the bravest of the children could not climb so high. "We'll not give up!" they warned. "Just you wait!"

"We will wait!" the skinny old man called back. "But we'll wait up here."

"And we'll wait down here!" the villagers replied.

At once they began to build new homes around the tree. Almost overnight, huts sprouted like giant mushrooms.

Days passed, with the villagers camped below and the old couple perched above. The old man and the old woman got so hungry that they chewed the leaves from the twigs and the twigs from the branches. They even gnawed bark from the trunk. The skinny old man got skinnier. The scrawny old woman got scrawnier. Their teeth grew long and sharp.

"How frightful!" they teased each other.

But they would not give back the *jimbu* shells.

Weeks passed. The villagers got angrier and angrier. "We'll smoke those two out like bees from a hive," they said. The villagers fanned the cooking fires inside their huts until smoke billowed through the roof holes.

The skinny old man's eyes smarted. The scrawny old woman sneezed. But they did not come down from the tree. Swinging the bag of shells between them, they climbed higher, past big-beaked hornbills and scolding gray parrots, to the airy boughs where the eagle perched.

"Hold on tight with your toes," the old man told the old woman.

Months passed, and the time of rains came. He shivered. Her teeth chattered. Then something strange began to happen to both of them. As the weather got wetter, the old man and old woman got hairier. Fur coats bristled on their backs, and fuzz covered their arms and legs. White hair frizzed on their faces, and tufts grew on the tops of their ears.

"You look beastly!" teased the scrawny old woman.

"Not so beastly as you!" the skinny old man retorted. "You're growing a tail!"

"A tail!" shrieked the old woman, twirling about to see for herself. Suddenly she stopped and pointed at him. "You've got a tail of your own! It's as plain as the beard on your chin!"

The old man gawked at her. She stared back, and both of them hooted with laughter. They jumped from limb to limb, trying to pull each other's tails. A flurry of leaves fell, and the sack of shells teetered back and forth on its branch.

Kerplunk! Kerplink! Plink! Plink! Plink!

Jimbu shells showered down on the huts below.

The skinny old man and the scrawny old woman stopped

screeching. They stopped playing tag. Still as carved statues, they watched the villagers scramble to pick up the shells.

Then the old man turned to the old woman. "It's all for the best," he said. "The *jimbus* do belong to them."

She nodded. "And seashells do not belong in trees."

"But we do!" they said together. "And we will not come down—not ever."

With a wave of their beautiful tails, the skinny old man and the scrawny old woman climbed up to the very crown of the tree. That's where they stayed, chattering to each other, playing tag, nibbling on new leaves, and napping in the sunshine.

In time, the villagers forgot why they had built their village beneath that particular tree. They even forgot that the old couple overhead were once their neighbors. They called them simply "People of the Trees."

◆ ◆

Give the monkey his branch of palm nuts.
MEANING: Don't take what isn't yours.
—*Bassa proverb, Ivory Coast*

◆ ◆ ◆ ◆ ◆ ◆ ◆ ◆ ◆ ◆ ◆ ◆ ◆ ◆ ◆ ◆ ◆ ◆ ◆ ◆

The Monkey, the Rats, the Cheese

• A CAPE VERDE ISLANDS TALE •

A patas monkey is sometimes called the military monkey because its bright orange face sports a large, regimental-style white mustache. But this long-legged monkey would rather run than fight. A patas monkey, the fastest-moving monkey in the world, reaches ground speeds of 35 miles an hour (56 kilometers an hour).

This story is from the Cape Verde Islands off the coast of Senegal in West Africa.

Once, two hungry rat brothers were hurrying home arm in arm. When they were almost there, they came upon a large, round cheese lying in the middle of the road.

"Finders, keepers!" squealed the older of the two brothers. He tried to pick up the cheese. "*Oof!*" he groaned. "It's too heavy!"

"Too much for one but not for two," said the younger brother. "If we divide the cheese, we can each take half."

The older rat wanted the whole thing for himself, but half a cheese was better than none. "All right," he agreed. "I'll cut it in two."

"Let me," said the younger rat. "Dividing it was my idea."

"But I saw it first," objected his brother.

The two rats glared at each other. Neither brother trusted the other to divide the cheese evenly. They sat down in the middle of the road and bickered while the cheese melted in the hot sun.

A patas monkey came loping along the road. When he saw the cheese, he skidded to a stop, and stared at the rats in surprise. "What's this? Two rats, a big cheese, and you're fighting?"

"We need to divide the cheese so that each of us gets the same," snapped the older rat.

"Exactly the same," added his brother.

"I'm sure I can put an end to your squabbles," said the monkey. "Wait here."

In no time, the patas monkey had fetched a large cleaver and split the cheese. But he did not cut it down the middle. One side was much larger than the other.

"Look what I did!" the monkey exclaimed. "This piece is much too big!" He began to nibble the larger side. "I'll just even it up."

The rat brothers watched in alarm as the patas monkey took bite after bite. "Stop!" cried both of them at once.

"Stop?" asked the monkey. "I can't do that. Now this piece is too little!"

The patas monkey gnawed on the other piece of the cheese until it was even smaller. "Don't worry," he told the rats. "I'll fix it."

"Please, Friend Monkey, don't do any more fixing," the older brother begged. "You've done quite enough already."

"Why, I never quit in the middle of a job!" mumbled the monkey around a mouthful of cheese.

The patas monkey moved from one piece of cheese to the other, taking a bite here and another there, but the halves were never even. Finally, only the rind was left.

"You ate all our cheese!" cried the rat brothers. "That's not fair!"

"What could be fairer?" asked the monkey. "Neither one of you has any cheese, so now you've nothing to quarrel about." He brushed the crumbs from his chin. "I told you I'd put an end to your squabbling."

"Listen . . . ," the older brother began.

"Don't bother to thank me," said the monkey. "I'm always happy to help." He waved good-bye and sped up the road.

The two rats watched him go but did not chase him. They knew better than to try to catch a patas monkey.

"Anyway," said the bigger brother, "if we find another cheese, we'll know what to do. One of us can cut it, and the other can have first choice."

"And neither of us will ask a monkey for help," added his brother.

Arm in arm, the two rats hurried home.

The Baboon and the Shark

◆ A FOLKTALE FROM LIBERIA ◆

Baboons, found throughout Africa, are sometimes called "dog-faced monkeys" because of their doglike appearance. In South Africa, baboons were trained to herd goats, and ancient Egyptians taught them to harvest dates from trees.

Although they're good climbers, baboons are ground monkeys. They usually travel in groups, but this baboon lives alone and is much too curious about others for his own good.

Once there was a curious young baboon. He was especially interested in the ocean. Each morning he left the grasslands and climbed a tall kola tree that overhung a quiet bay. From here, he could watch the fish swim in the sea while he ate his breakfast of plantains and peas. When he was through, he shook his *kinjah*, the sack that held his breakfast, and sent a shower of peas into the water below.

Swarms of small fish gobbled up the peas. They, in turn, were swallowed by a school of middle-size fish. These were snapped up by a big fish, which then vanished in the yawning jaws of a great gray shark.

"Thank you kindly, Brother Baboon," said the shark when he had swallowed the last one. "You are truly good-hearted."

The baboon gazed with envy as the shark swam about in lazy circles. "Are there others in the ocean like you?" he asked.

"Few fish are as large, and none as handsome," replied the shark. "Listen, and I'll tell you some secrets of the sea."

Soon the young baboon's head was stuffed with tales of flying fish and singing dolphins, of stingrays and eight-armed octopuses, of King Lobster and his pearl-and-coral palace.

"If you would teach me to swim, I could see for myself," the baboon said wistfully.

"You? Swim?" scoffed the shark. "You'd sink like a stone. Better watch me instead."

The shark dove, disappearing in the blue-green water. The baboon watched but saw only ripples. He listened but heard only the swish of waves. He did not hear the uproar that greeted the shark at the bottom of the sea.

Electric eels were sparking, and the dogfish barking.

The catfish were yowling, and the wolf-fish howling.

The sea horse was neighing, and the cowfish bawling.

The commotion confused the shark. "What's happening?" he cried.

"Use your eyes!" scolded a cross old crab. "Can't you see that the king is ill?"

Then the shark noticed that King Lobster sat slumped on his throne. His claws dangled, his feelers drooped, and his shiny green shell had turned bright red. Fish of all sizes surrounded their king, moaning and churning the water with their fins.

"That racket won't help," grumbled the old crab. "Only a monkey's heart can cure King Lobster."

"A monkey's heart!" chorused the fish. "Give the king a monkey's heart!"

"I know a good-hearted baboon," the shark shouted over the din. "Perhaps he can pay our king a visit."

"The sooner the better," snapped an oyster, closing his shell to shut out the noise.

◆ ◆ ◆ ◆

When the shark returned to the bay the next morning, he found the young baboon perched in the kola tree, just where he'd left him.

"I've been thinking," said the shark. "You're so curious about the ocean, it's only fair that you see it for yourself."

"I can't go in the water," the baboon objected. "You said I would sink like a stone."

"You can ride on my back, Brother Baboon."

"I'd better not . . . ," the baboon began.

The shark smiled, showing a double row of knife-sharp teeth. "You're not afraid?" he said.

"Not me!" Tying his *kinjah* to a tree branch, the baboon jumped nimbly onto the shark's back.

At first the monkey enjoyed his sail, shouting to seagulls above and wishing on starfish below. But when they got so

far from shore that the kola tree looked no taller than a pea plant, the baboon began to be nervous. "I think it's time to turn back, Friend Shark," he said.

"Oh, no! Not yet. King Lobster wants to meet you," answered the shark.

"Me?" asked the baboon in surprise.

"He's very eager. He needs . . . ," the shark hesitated, ". . . to eat you."

The baboon almost lost his grip on the shark's slippery fin. "Eat me?"

"Oh, not all of you," the shark reassured him. "The king just needs your heart to make him well."

"But my heart's my most important part!"

"Of course." The shark snorted. "That's why it's good medicine."

The baboon didn't dare to scratch his head to help his thinking. He needed both hands to hold on. If he let go, he would drown. "I can't go on," he moaned. "I haven't the heart for it!"

"What?" The shark stopped swimming. "You haven't a heart?"

"I mean . . . ," the baboon said quickly, "I mean I don't have it with me."

"Then where is it?" demanded the shark.

"My heart's in my *kinjah*, hanging in the kola tree. I didn't know I'd be needing it."

"How stupid!" shouted the shark. "You monkeys really are foolish fellows. We will have to go back for it."

Whirling around, the shark swam so fast that the salt flew from the water. The baboon squeezed his eyes shut, too terrified to look, until they'd reached the bay again.

The shark glared at the baboon's sack, hanging high overhead. "Go get it," he ordered.

"Yes," the baboon agreed. "I'm going right now."

The baboon scampered up the kola tree, past the branch where his *kinjah* was tied, and climbed, limb by limb, to the very top of the tree.

"Hurry up," insisted the shark.

"Patience!" called the baboon.

The sun dropped down to the sea and the moon rolled up in the sky. "It's getting dark," the shark complained.

"Then good night, Friend Shark. No need to wait any longer."

The shark thought the monkey's voice sounded very faint and far away. Alarmed, he cried, "But where is your heart?"

"Beating in my chest, where it belongs."

The shark was furious. He butted his head against the rocks and thrashed his tail until the water was white with froth. But at last he had to swim back to King Lobster's pearl-and-coral palace without the monkey . . . or his heart.

Although the shark came back to the bay each morning, he never again saw the baboon. From then on, that monkey stayed in the grasslands with his own kind. The curious young baboon had learned all he cared to know about the secrets of the sea.

◆ ◆

If a baboon wants to whistle, don't stop him.
MEANING: If someone wants to do the impossible,
let him find out for himself.
—Gola proverb, West Africa

◆ ◆

Monkey Ancestors

♦ LEMURS IN MADAGASCAR ♦

The name lemur *comes from a Latin word that means "ghostly spirit."*

Lemurs once thrived everywhere. Thirty-five million years ago, similiar monkey ancestors even lived in what is now the United States. But as the weather began to get colder, the lemurs began to disappear. Now they are found in just one area: Madagascar and its nearby islands in the Indian Ocean. So if you're looking for a lemur today, then you'll have to travel to Madagascar to see one.

For many millions of years, Madagascar was part of a huge African continent. Then, about 150 million years ago, it broke away and drifted more than 200 miles offshore. Today that chunk of land is known as Madagascar. It's about the size of the state of Texas and is the fourth-largest island in the world.

Madagascar acted as a lifeboat for lemurs and saved them from extinction. Lemurs living elsewhere did not fare so well. Wherever monkeys and lemurs shared the same area, the lemurs disappeared. Monkeys, with more highly developed brains, took over as the masters of the trees. But no monkeys got to Madagascar. The channel that stretches between Africa and the island is too wide for monkeys to swim across.

Another kind of primate did reach the island. The first people arrived there some 1,500 years ago. They didn't come from Africa, as you might guess, but sailed across the ocean from Malaysia. These settlers called themselves the Malagasy, and that's how people in the Republic of Madagascar are known today.

From the first, the Malagasy were both fascinated and frightened by lemurs. Although lemurs are shy tree dwellers, some look or sound quite scary, and almost all of them are nighttime prowlers. As they search for food, their huge eyes glow in the dark like lanterns, and the forest shakes with their bone-chilling shrieks and moans. Although most present-day lemurs aren't much larger than house cats, when the Malagasy arrived, they found some the size of gorillas. No wonder they thought meeting a lemur was bad luck!

Lucky you, if you get a glimpse of one of these lemurs:

+ A **gray mouse lemur** is the smallest living member of the species. Your breakfast egg is probably bigger. A mouse lemur weighs only two or three ounces. A mother lemur carries her tiny twins in her mouth for their first three weeks of life.

- The **white-footed sportive lemur** is a timid, one-pound vegetarian. But when it's threatened, it rears up on its hind legs and lifts its hands like a boxer ready to punch an attacker.

- A **ring-tailed lemur** looks dressed for a clown act in the circus. It has black smudges about its eyes, a black triangular nose, and a black-and-white-striped tail as long as a bathrobe belt. Ringtails use their tails to send messages, waving them back and forth like signal flags. A male lemur finds his tail quite handy in a "stink fight." He rubs it across the scent glands on his wrists and then, with flicks of his tail, throws the scent at his opponent. A "stink fight" can last for an hour, but no one gets hurt. The winner is whoever smells best—or least—at the end.

- Leaping lemurs! What was that? Most likely it was a **sifaka**. Sifakas use their powerful hind legs to bound from tree to tree like flying kangaroos. On the ground, a sifaka's bouncy hops look more like dance steps. Like all lemurs, a sifaka has a sharp sense of smell. If it sees or smells danger, it shrieks, "Sifak! Sifak!" That's how it got its name. Legend says that a sifaka doesn't drink water but licks the dew from its fur when it's thirsty.

- The largest of today's lemurs is the **indri**. It's four feet tall but weighs only twelve pounds. When the Malagasy first saw them, they thought that indris were the ghosts of their ancestors. Since these lemurs like to sunbathe, the Malagasy believed that they must be descended from a race of sun worshipers.

The indri got its name from Malagasy tour guides pointing to it and shouting, "Indri! Indri!" European visitors thought this was the lemur's name, but the guides were simply shouting, "Look! Look!"

The native name for an indri is *babakota*, but this lemur's mournful howl has earned it the title "dog of the forest." Another reason for its nickname is that an indri can be trained to search and retrieve like a hunting dog.

The Malagasy believe that the indri teach their young to leap through the trees by tossing them back and forth.

Another old superstition says that if you throw a spear at an indri, it will catch it and throw it back at you. You might miss, but an indri wouldn't!

According to legend, plants found in an indri's nest will cure any illness.

The Malagasy still look on indris with awe. These lemurs are never intentionally killed, and a dead one is always buried with honor.

♦ The **aye-aye** gets it name from its shrill, eerie cry. Only the size of a house cat, it's the most feared of the lemurs. An aye-aye looks patched together from scraps of other animals. At first glance, it might be a large squirrel with sharp rodent's teeth and grizzled brown fur like rusty steel wool. It has oversize, protruding batlike ears, a pointed snout like a fox, enormous yellow owl eyes, and a puffy tail like an ostrich feather. But its worst feature is its witchlike, bony black fingers. The long middle finger is as thin as a piece of wire, and like wire, the aye-aye can bend it in any direction. It uses this special finger to dig for insects in tree trunks and poke holes in coconuts so it can drink the milk.

Aye-aye Lemur

The Malagasy believe an aye-aye can bewitch you. If it points its middle finger in your direction, you'll die a dreadful death. Until recently, the Malagasy so feared the aye-ayes that they killed any that appeared in a village. Even now, the sight of one makes people flee their homes.

The aye-aye is one of the most threatened of the lemurs. It's in danger of becoming Madagascar's newest and noisiest ghostly spirit.

TOP: Ring-Tailed Lemur
MIDDLE LEFT: Ring-Tailed Lemur MIDDLE RIGHT: Sifaka
BOTTOM: Ring-Tailed Lemur

FROM LEFT: Indri, White-Footed Sportive Lemur, Baby Gray Mouse Lemur
BOTTOM: Gray Mouse Lemur

✦ Speaking of Monkeys ✦

You don't need to meet a monkey to speak monkey talk. Monkeys often pop up in everyday conversations. Maybe you've used some of these monkey-talk words or phrases yourself.

If you're up to some monkey business, you're into mischief.

Someone who makes a monkey out of you makes you look silly.

Don't be a copycat, or someone might say, "Monkey see, monkey do."

If you monkey around with your food (or anything else), you're playing with it.

When you cut a monkeyshine, you're performing or showing off.

When you've got your monkey up, you're angry, but when you've had a great time, you've had more fun than a barrel of monkeys!

Surprised? Just say, "Well, I'll be a monkey's uncle!"

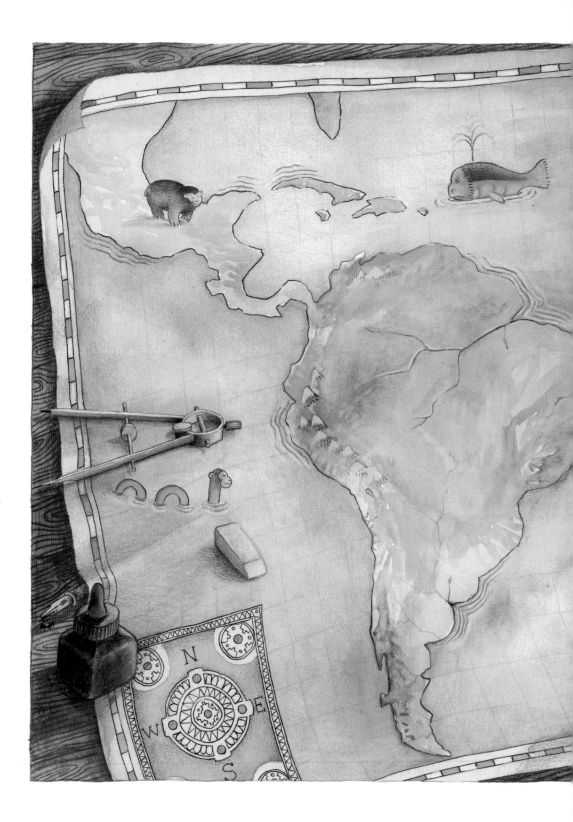

Monkeys in the Americas

The First Monkeys

◆ A MYTH FROM MEXICO ◆

Capuchins are small monkeys with big brains. Of all the New World monkeys, they are the most like humans. They scowl, grin, make faces, and even pucker their lips and make kissing noises when they're courting. But capuchins also do something no human can do. They swing by their tail!

The monkeys in this old Mayan myth are probably the clever little capuchins.

In the beginning, Hurakan the wind swept through a bare and empty universe. Then Hurakan bellowed, "Earth!" and the earth appeared. Different gods took on the difficult task of finishing it. Water gods scooped out lakes and rivers and filled them with fish. Land gods made mountains and valleys and added winged birds and four-legged beasts.

"You forgot the most important," scolded Itzamna, Ruler of the Heavens and of Day and Night. "The earth needs people."

At once, some of the gods set about carving men and women from sticks of wood. The stick men were quite stiff and not very big, but they were able to hunt and to till the

corn and beans. The stick women were even smaller, yet they could cook the food and care for the animals. So Itzamna was satisfied with the gods' creations.

Most satisfied of all were the wooden people themselves. They became so proud and boastful that they ignored the gods who'd made them. That angered Itzamna.

"We must teach those stick people a lesson," he declared.

So Yum Kaax, the god of corn, withered the ears on the stalks. The gods of the red bean and the black bean and the white bean caused the pods to rot. The rain god, Chac, emptied his water gourd again and again until the land was flooded.

But the stick people just shrugged. "Don't blame us," they said.

Such boldness enraged the gods. They turned everything on earth against the wooden people.

The men's spears grew dull, and their hoes lay down in the field. "We will not work for you again," said the tools.

The women's cooking pots cracked and spilled. "Too bad!" the pots jeered. "You chipped us! You burned us!"

Their own animals chased the stick people. When they scrambled to safety on housetops, the roofs crumbled beneath their feet. When they climbed the trees in the forest, the branches shook them down. Even the mountain caves closed before the stick people. There was no escape.

"Stick people were a mistake," agreed the gods who looked after the earth.

"Try again," Itzamna told them. "Make different people."

The gods did. This time they crafted men and women from ripe ears of corn. These corn dolls worked hard. They cared for the land and the animals and respected the gods.

Itzamna nodded. "Good!" he said.

For a thousand years, the corn people thrived. Then something surprising began to happen. The corn people started to change. The changes came slowly. First, bones replaced corncobs. Then skin replaced corn husks, and real hair replaced corn silk. In time, all the corn people had been magically transformed. They looked much as people do today, and that was pleasing to the gods.

But in their hurry to be rid of the stick people, the gods had been careless. They had overlooked a small wooden man and a small wooden woman clinging to a tree in the jungle. These last two stick people were afraid to come down. They hid in the treetops for so long that they grew tails to help them hold on to the limbs.

Their children, their grandchildren, and those who came after them lived in the trees as well. They grew tails, too, and fur covered their wooden bodies. Nothing remained to show that once they'd been stiff little stick people.

According to the Mayans of long ago, they had become the first monkeys.

The Spider Monkey's Close Shave

◆ A BRAZILIAN FOLKTALE ◆

Spider monkeys earned their name from the way they run, holding their arms and legs at an angle, much like the bent legs of a spider. But spider monkeys are at their best when swinging through trees. They leap from limb to limb like trapeze artists, using their long tail like another hand. To help them hold on, spider monkeys have no hair on the end of their tail.

Spider monkeys are widespread in Central America and South America, and so are variations of this story.

Once, in the middle of a rain forest, there lived a fun-loving spider monkey. Sometimes he swung with other monkeys in the trees. Sometimes he played hide-and-seek among the leaves. Sometimes, just for fun, he sent a shower of palm nuts down on the prowling puma below.

One morning the spider monkey wanted something different to do. He sat on a branch, thinking and chewing the tip of his long furry tail. "I'm tired of monkey tricks," he said. "I want to do some people things."

The spider monkey swung through the forest until he reached the river. Nearby was a road, and overlooking it was a tall mahogany tree. "Ah!" cried the monkey, climbing up the tree. "Just right for people watching!"

Soon the spider monkey saw an old woman balancing a large basket of clothes on her head. "I'm going to the river to wash these clothes," she told him. "If you will carry my basket, I will give you a bath, too."

The spider monkey shook his head. "No, thank you," he answered. "I like water, but I don't like baths."

Next the spider monkey saw a boy in a straw hat pushing a wheelbarrow up the road. It was piled high with melons.

"If you will help me push," the boy told him, "I will let you taste my melons."

The spider monkey shook his head. "No, thank you," he answered. "I like melons, but I don't like work."

After the boy had gone, the monkey noticed a small building across the road. A line of bearded men waited outside the door.

"Something fun must be happening inside," said the spider monkey, "and I want to find out what."

The monkey jumped down from the tree and joined the line. Each time the door swung open, a man went inside. Each time, the monkey heard him say, "Give me a shave!"

When the man came out again, his chin whiskers were gone and his cheeks were as smooth as the skin of a mango.

"That's what I'd like!" the spider monkey said to himself. "I want to be handsome, too."

At last the spider monkey got his turn. Like all the others, he strutted inside and sat down on the high stool. "Give me a shave," he told the man.

The barber stared at the hairy spider monkey. "I don't know where to begin," he said.

The spider monkey scowled. "Give me a shave!" he repeated.

"I could trim your tail a little," the barber suggested. He soaped his brush, caught hold of the spider monkey's tail, and covered it with lather.

The brush tickled. "Hee! Hee! Hee!" tittered the monkey.

The barber laughed, too. With one stroke of his razor, he shaved off the hair from the end of the spider monkey's tail. "How's that?"

The monkey peered over his shoulder. The last twelve inches of his tail were as bare as snake's skin. "Eeek!" cried the spider monkey, hopping up and down. "Give me back my hair!"

The barber stuck some of the hair back on with soap, but when the monkey twitched his tail, it all fell off again.

"You took my hair!" cried the spider monkey. "Now give me your razor. That's only fair."

Without waiting for an answer, he snatched the barber's razor. Then, holding his tail straight up in the air like a flagpole without a flag, the spider monkey ran out the door and down the road. He ran until he came upon a fisherwoman sitting on the riverbank, cleaning a fine, fat catfish.

"Fishing looks like fun," said the spider monkey.

"Catching fish is fun," agreed the woman. "Cleaning fish isn't. I've only an old wooden scraper to do the job."

"Try this." The monkey held out his razor. "This blade can shave the whiskers off a catfish."

The woman took the razor and started to scrape her fish, but the scales were thick and the blade was thin. With a sharp crack, the razor snapped in two.

"Look what you've done!" shouted the spider monkey, hopping up and down.

"I didn't mean to," said the fisherwoman.

"You broke my razor," cried the spider monkey. "Now give me your fish. That's only fair."

Without waiting for an answer, he wrapped his tail around the catfish and bounded down the road with it. The spider monkey did not stop until he came to the house of a baker. The baker was just taking a big pan of corn bread from his outdoor oven.

"Mmmm!" the spider monkey said, sniffing. "Corn bread tastes good with catfish."

"So it does," agreed the baker. He eyed the monkey's fish and smacked his lips. "I could cook that catfish in my oven."

"Please do," said the spider monkey, tossing the fish to the baker with a flick of his tail. "I'll go catch another."

The monkey skipped down to the river and dangled the bare tip of his tail in the water. He waited and waited, but the only bite he got was from a large snapping turtle. "Ow!" squealed the spider monkey. "Fishing is *not* fun!"

The spider monkey shook the water from his tail and stamped back to the baker's house.

"You were right," the baker told the spider monkey, licking his fingers. "The catfish was delicious."

"What?" cried the spider monkey. "You ate my fish?"

"You gave it to me," the baker protested.

"I let you borrow it," said the monkey.

"But . . . ," the baker began.

"You took my fish!" shouted the spider monkey, hopping up and down. "Now give me a sack of your flour. That's only fair."

The baker just laughed, so the spider monkey twisted his tail around a big sack of flour. He darted down the road with it, away from the river and the fisherwoman and the baker and the snapping turtle. But the sack was heavy, and the spider monkey's tail was sore. He stopped to rest outside a tumbledown hut. Suddenly the door burst open, and five little girls spilled out.

"Mama! Mama!" called the smallest one. "Come see the funny monkey with the long bare tail!"

The spider monkey bowed politely. "It's much more useful without hair," he said. He unwound his tail from the sack. "Maybe your mama can make cakes with this flour."

"Cakes!" squealed the little girls in delight.

The smallest girl went to find her mother, her four sisters went to find flat baking stones, and the monkey went to find a quiet tree for a nap.

The spider monkey was so tired that he did not wake up until almost sundown. When he returned to the hut, the mother and her five daughters were waiting for him.

"Kindly give me my sack of flour," said the spider monkey.

"It's gone," the mother replied. "I used it to make cakes."

"Then give me a cake," said the monkey.

"They're gone, too," said the mother. "The girls ate them."

The spider monkey hopped up and down. "You used up all the flour? You ate up all the cakes?" he shrieked. "Then I'll take one of your daughters. That's only fair."

The spider monkey scooped up the smallest girl with his tail and dashed down the road.

"Stop!" cried the mother, running after them.

But the monkey moved so fast that even a jaguar could not have caught him. Soon he was back in the forest and swinging in the treetops again.

"Put me down," ordered the girl.

The spider monkey was surprised. "Swinging's fun!"

"Not for me," she said. "I'm going to be sick."

"Do you want to play hide-and-seek?" asked the spider monkey.

"You could find me," she said, "but I'd never find you."

"Let's throw palm nuts at the puma," the monkey suggested.

"No, no, no!" scolded the little girl. "A puma is a kitty."

"Then what do you want to do?" asked the spider monkey.

The girl looked about. The forest was dark and shadowy, and nearby an owl began to hoot. "I want to go home," she said.

Now that he thought about it, that's what the spider monkey wanted, too.

"Fair enough," he agreed and took the little girl home.

After that, the spider monkey was content to stay in the rain forest. But the hair on his tail never did grow back. To this day, the end of a spider monkey's tail is bare. It's a reminder of the close shave that one of them once had with a human.

❖ ❖

The monkey does not put its paw into the jaguar's mouth twice.
MEANING: Experience is the best teacher.
—Proverb, Ecuador

❖ ❖

So Say the Little Monkeys

◆ A TALE FROM AMAZONIA ◆

Amazonia is the name of the huge rain forest that borders the Amazon River in Brazil, Peru, and Ecuador. It is the home of many species of monkey. Among the most numerous are the small squirrel monkeys. Although they cannot hang by their tails, squirrel monkeys use them for balance and wrap them around their shoulders to keep dry when it rains.

In Brazil, when something is put off until tomorrow that should be done today, people repeat the proverb: "Amanhã. So say the little monkeys."

Troops of squirrel monkeys live along the riverbanks in Brazil. So long as the sun shines, they scamper in the tree-tops, chattering "Chee! Chee! Chee!" The younger squirrel monkeys dangle by one arm above the coffee-colored water and tease the hungry alligators that hope a monkey may drop in for dinner.

But when the sun sets, when rain pours from the dark sky and the wind tries to tumble them from their perches, the young monkeys pull their tails over their heads and cry "Brrr! Brrr!" Throughout the long night, the squirrel mon-

keys huddle together and squabble over which ones deserve the drier places in the middle.

"*Amanhã*," an older squirrel monkey tells them. "Tomorrow we will build houses to keep out the rain."

"They will be snug houses," promises another, "with thick, leafy roofs to keep you dry."

"They will be strong houses," a third boasts. "No wind will blow them down."

"They will be safe houses," adds a fourth, "high in the trees above the alligators."

All the older monkeys nod and look wise. "Those are the houses we will build tomorrow."

But when they wake up to a sunny morning, the squirrel monkeys forget how wet and miserable they've been. The bigger monkeys stuff their mouths with fruit. The smaller monkeys spring from branch to branch and call to the jaguar hiding in the underbrush, "Yah! Yah! Can't catch us!"

Suddenly one of the young ones stops. "Is it time to build houses yet?" he asks.

"Who needs a house when the sun shines?" scoffs an old monkey.

"*Amanhã*," chorus the other old ones. "Tomorrow is soon enough. We will make houses *amanhã*."

Day after day, year after year, the squirrel monkeys still wait for tomorrow.

◆ Traveling Monkeys ◆

Many monkeys love the water and can do their own version of the dog paddle. But none of them can swim long distances, so if a monkey's found across a stretch of open water, someone brought it there—either on purpose or by mistake.

Monkeys have been world travelers for a long time. In the Middle Ages, some sailors brought pet monkeys aboard vessels for companionship during the weeks at sea. Small and easily cared for, most made good shipmates. But a few sailors believed that a monkey aboard a boat invited bad luck. If a sudden storm arose, or the ship was becalmed, they thought the monkey must be to blame. Some seamen refused to set foot on a boat if a monkey was on board. Even today, fears and superstitions persist that a monkey at sea means trouble.

Three hundred fifty years ago, a half dozen African green monkeys became unexpected passengers on a vessel sailing to Barbados. Perhaps they were pets that had escaped from their owner. Perhaps they were wild vervets that had managed to hide in the ship's hold. All that is known about these long-tailed "stowaways" is that, at the end of the voyage, they scampered off in Barbados. Old World monkeys had crossed the ocean to live in a New World paradise.

The fur on the backs of African vervets, or green monkeys, shines olive green in the sunlight, and that's how they got their name. Vervets are as nimble on the ground as they are in trees. They can run, trot, or even gallop like a dog, and they're great jumpers. No wonder these monkeys were difficult to catch or corral!

Today, descendants of that handful of vervets aboard that long-ago ship from West Africa number 10,000. Although the Barbados government tries to restrict them to the Wildlife Reserve, they still wander the small island in groups of a dozen or so and make midnight raids on farmers' vegetable gardens. Like many of us, vervets are especially fond of tender new potatoes.

Tasi and the Oranges

♦ A BRAZILIAN INDIAN FOLKTALE ♦

Howler monkeys live in rain forests from Mexico to Argentina. Wary of humans, howlers hide in treetops and are seldom seen. But these big monkeys are some of the noisiest creatures on earth. Each morning they shake the forest with thundering booms and bellows that can be heard for miles.

To the ancient Mayan people of Central America, howlers were sacred. More recently the Wayana farmers of Brazil think of these monkeys as pests.

Once there was a red-furred howler monkey named Tasi. Her name is the Wayana Indian word for "sister."

Tasi lived with her mother and a dozen howler aunts, uncles, and cousins in the leafy canopy of the rain forest. From her perch high in a brazilwood tree, Tasi looked down on a nearby orange grove. She could see the bright oranges dotting the branches and could sniff their nose-tingling scent.

One morning Tasi said, "I want to taste an orange."

"Don't even think about it!" shrieked her mother.

"Remember your father," warned her aunts.

"The farmer might catch you!" growled her uncles.

So Tasi just gazed at the orange grove from her treetop. Each day she saw the farmer bring an empty basket into the orchard. Each day she watched him fill it with fruit.

"The farmer doesn't get here until the sun is high," Tasi said to herself. "I could pick an orange before he comes."

The next day Tasi woke early, before the first bellbird started to sing. The other howlers still slept, grasping the tree limbs with their tails.

Quietly Tasi climbed down the brazilwood tree and crept on all fours into the orchard. Quickly she scrambled up an orange tree and snatched the ripest fruit.

Tasi sniffed it. "Ah!"

Tasi nibbled it. "Mmmm!"

Tasi was about to take a big bite, when she heard "Stop!"

The farmer ran toward her. "Get out!" he shouted, shaking a hoe. "Or I'll get you!"

Tasi dropped the orange, jumped to the ground, and scuttled back to the forest. After that, she stayed in the treetops with the rest of her family and ate leaves.

But Tasi couldn't forget how delicious the orange had smelled, and she couldn't keep her eyes from the orchard. She saw the farmer arrive each morning and watched him leave with his basket full of fruit each afternoon.

"I could visit the orchard after the farmer has gone," Tasi said to herself, "and he'd never know I'd been there."

At sundown that evening, after her family had settled for the night but before any tree frogs began to croak, Tasi slipped into the orange grove. She stopped beneath the nearest tree and stretched her hand toward the biggest orange.

Zeeeee! Something whistled past her ear.

Tasi whirled about. Standing in the shadows was the farmer. This time the farmer wasn't waving a hoe. This time he was holding a blowgun.

"Now I've got you!" he shouted. He pushed another dart into the long bamboo tube and raised it to his mouth. "Just you wait!"

Tasi didn't wait. She ran as fast as she could back to her brazilwood tree.

Safe at home, Tasi thought about her father. He had gone into the orange grove, too, and had never come back. She might not be so lucky again.

For three days, Tasi did not even peek at the orchard. She pinched her nose so she wouldn't smell the oranges. But early on the fourth morning, she happened to look down just as the farmer arrived with his basket. Today it wasn't empty. The farmer reached in and pulled something out.

"It's a little man!" exclaimed Tasi. "The farmer's got a friend!"

The farmer shinnied up an orange tree and balanced the man on a shady branch. "Now, keep watch!" he called loudly.

When the birds saw the stranger sitting in the orange tree, they squawked and flew away. But Tasi laughed aloud. The little man looked too funny to be frightening.

The man's face was as pale as a fish bone. His eyes bulged, and his nose was as long and green as a caiman's. His legs were short, his arms were stubby, and stringy brown hair straggled from beneath his hat.

"You scare birds away, but you can't scare me!" Tasi cried.

The little man smiled.

Tasi swung down from her tree. Cautiously she crept into the orchard and squinted up at the small man in the tree. "Would you please pick an orange for me?" she asked politely.

The little man smiled in answer.

"If you give me an orange, we will be friends," said Tasi.

The little man did not reply.

"GIVE ME AN ORANGE!" Tasi repeated loudly.

The little man stared straight ahead and kept smiling.

Tasi jumped up and down. "Look at me!"

She scrambled up the orange tree until she reached the branch where the little man sat. Raising her right hand, she pinched his cheek. "That's for being rude!" said Tasi.

Although she had scarcely touched him, her fingers stuck fast to his face. "Let go!" Tasi demanded.

The little man sat as stiff and silent as before.

Tasi puffed with anger. With her left hand, she knocked off the little man's hat. The hat tumbled to the ground, but her hand was stuck in the man's wispy hair. Still he smiled.

"Stop grinning at me!" Tasi cried, and poked him with her toe.

The little man wobbled a bit, but now her toe was stuck, too. No matter how hard she jiggled, Tasi could not free her foot. "Let me go!"

Tasi thought she heard the small man snicker. Holding tight to the limb with her tail, she kicked with her other foot. The man rocked back and forth on the branch. Tasi rocked with him, for now both her hands and both her feet were caught. "Help!" she called.

No one heard her. Tasi's mother and her aunts and her uncles and her cousins were sound asleep in the brazilwood tree. Tasi knew she had to help herself. She took a big breath, squeezed her eyes shut, and shook the branch so hard that all the oranges fell from the tree.

With a loud crack, the limb broke. Tasi fell, too, still stuck fast to the little man. Both of them tumbled headlong onto a fire-ant mound below.

The ants tickled Tasi's nose. "Ah-ah-choo!" she sneezed.

The ants stung Tasi's ears. "Ooooh!" she wailed.

She couldn't lift a hand to swat the ants. She couldn't lift a foot to step on them. She couldn't even roll over. "Wow! Wow! Wow!" howled Tasi.

Beside her, the little man lay as silent as a stone. The fire ants didn't make him yell. They didn't even make him twitch.

Tasi stopped in the middle of a howl. "Is something wrong?" she asked him. When she twisted her neck to get a better look at the little man, she saw that everything about him was wrong.

His nose, which broke in the fall, was nothing more than squash from the farmer's garden. One of his eyes was missing, and the other was just a peach pit. His straggly hair was corn silk, and only three teeth remained in his smile.

"And they are nothing but pumpkin seeds!" Tasi exclaimed.

Then, without a sound, the little man began to move. First one ear, then the other trickled down his neck. His fingers and toes started running together. Soon his arms and legs were melting, too.

Tasi watched in amazement as the little man disappeared before her eyes. He left only a sticky puddle behind. "I believe you're made of beeswax!" she cried.

Tasi wiggled her fingers in the soft wax. Suddenly she realized that she was no longer stuck. She pulled one hand away and then the other. She shook her left foot free, next her right foot. Stiff from ears to tail, her soft red fur gummy with wax, Tasi hobbled back to the brazilwood tree and climbed to the top. "I'll never come down again," she vowed.

And she never did. But she never forgot the little wax man or the fire ants, either. Each morning, when the sun shone in the sky like a big, bright orange, Tasi puffed out her cheeks and bellowed, louder than any howler monkey ever had before, "WOW! WOW! WOW!"

◆ *When Is a Monkey Not a Monkey?* ◆

Although most English-speaking countries don't have native monkeys, they have expressions that include "monkey." Seven of them are listed below. Try to guess what these monkey expressions mean.

1. Where would you eat a "monkey nut"?

2. What is "monkey pie"?

3. Where might you see a "monkey bear"?

4. Where would you find a "grease monkey"?

5. Why would you be happy to have a "monkey" in your piggy bank?

6. A "monkey dodger" isn't a zookeeper. What does he do?

7. You've reached the top when you're on "monkey island," but where are you?

◆ ◆ ◆ ◆

ANSWERS

1. You'd eat "monkey nuts" in England. It's slang for peanuts.

2. "Monkey pie" is a nickname for coconut cream pie in the United States.

3. A koala is sometimes called a "monkey bear" in Australia.

4. If you live in the United States or Canada, visit an car repair shop to see a "grease monkey." That's slang for an auto or airplane mechanic.

5. You've struck it rich! In Great Britain, a "monkey" is slang for 500 pounds, and a pound is a British unit of money worth more than a dollar.

6. A worker on a sheep farm in Australia is called a "monkey dodger."

7. You're at sea! The top tier of a ship's bridge is called "monkey island."

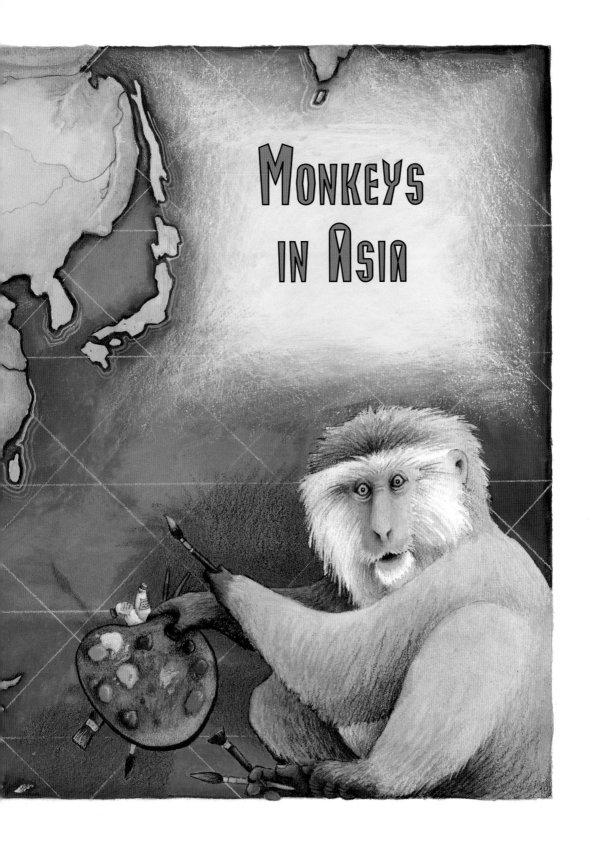

Monkeys in Asia

THE MONKEY KEEPER

• A CHINESE PARABLE •

It's not just what you do, but how you do it.
—*Lie Zi,* FOURTH CENTURY A.D.

In the land of Sung, there once was a monkey keeper in charge of ten especially handsome monkeys. He loved them like his own children. Each day he gave each monkey eight plump chestnuts. But one year, after a season of bad weather and bad luck, the keeper ran short of chestnuts.

"I am sorry," he told his monkeys, "but now I can give each of you only three nuts in the morning and four in the afternoon."

Hearing that, the monkeys hissed and howled. They shook the bars of their bamboo enclosure, bared their teeth, and threw their food bowl at the monkey keeper. Terrified, he ran and hid. But when the monkeys saw him again the next day, the man was smiling.

"Forgive me," their keeper said. "I was mistaken. I can give you four chestnuts in the morning, as always, and then you each shall get three more every afternoon."

"Aaaah," exclaimed the monkeys. They grinned at one another, pleased with their keeper once more.

◆ Monkey Sign Language ◆

If a monkey's lucky, it may live for twenty-five years. But there are three special Japanese macaque monkeys who have been around for at least a millennium and are still going strong.

You'll probably recognize this trio of monkeys, for they're often pictured on postcards or printed on T-shirts. Sometimes they decorate paperweights or bookends. Each monkey has a Japanese name, but we know them best as the Three Wise Monkeys. Their advice about getting along with others is understood everywhere, for they speak sign language with their hands.

Kikazaru covers his ears with his hands so he won't hear something he shouldn't. His message is HEAR NO EVIL.

Iwazaru claps his hands over his mouth so he won't say the wrong thing. His message is SPEAK NO EVIL.

Mizaru holds his hands over his eyes so he won't see anything bad. His message is SEE NO EVIL.

The saying about the monkeys' wisdom, and how they shared it, most likely originated in China and was brought to Japan by Buddhist monks more than a thousand years ago. Since the three monkeys were thought to watch over other voyagers, too, their likeness was chiseled on stone markers alongside country roads in Japan. Even today, some travelers stop and rub the monkeys for good luck and a safe journey.

Above the stable of the sacred horse in Nikko, Japan, is the most famous carving of the three monkeys. For 350 years, the Three Wise Monkeys have welcomed visitors to the shrine with their special sign language.

The Snow Monkey and the Boar

◆ A STORY OF OLD JAPAN ◆

The tale of the snow monkey and the boar was a favorite of the hanashika, *the Japanese storyteller. The monkey in the story is a snow monkey, a red-faced, short-tailed Japanese macaque. It lives the farthest north of any monkey in the world. In cold winter weather, these lively monkeys warm up by bathing in hot springs. They even wash their ears!*

In long-ago Japan, in a place named Shushin, there once lived a man and a snow monkey. They were partners.

The man was a traveling musician. He wandered from village to village, coaxing tunes from his three-stringed guitar. The snow monkey was an acrobat. While the man plucked the strings of his *samisen*, the monkey twirled and pranced, teetered on stilts, and turned cartwheels and backward somersaults. When he'd finished his performance, the crowd cheered. *"Banzai!"* they shouted. "Hurrah!" Many threw copper coins and a few tossed silver *bu* into the monkey's round straw hat.

◆ ◆ ◆ ◆

Many years before, on a frosty winter morning, the musician had found the snow monkey high in the mountains. His teeth were chattering from the cold, and he was so small, he scarcely had any tail at all. The man buttoned the shivering little monkey inside his padded jacket and carried him home to his wife.

"He's just a baby!" she exclaimed. "He needs us to care for him."

From then on, the snow monkey lived with the musician and his wife. They called him Taro, which was a name often given to a first son. The woman fed him miso soup and stuffed dumplings, and Taro grew bigger. The man taught him to dance and do tricks, and every day Taro grew more

clever as well. He soon understood almost every word the man and woman said, although Taro's own squeaks and squeals made no sense to them.

After a dozen years, a son was born to the musician and his wife. All three—man, woman, and monkey—were delighted.

"We shall name our son Bokuden, after the famous samurai," declared the man.

"Perhaps he, too, will become a warrior," said his wife.

Taro just grinned.

Like all babies, Bokuden cried. But he howled, he fussed, and he whimpered more than most, for he soon learned that even his smallest wail would bring his parents running.

"Do something!" they begged Taro.

Then the snow monkey turned somersaults or made silly faces until, to everyone's relief, the baby stopped crying.

Performing in villages by day and amusing the baby at night began to wear Taro out. Already the hair on his head was sprinkled with white like mountain frost. He grew as skinny as a skeleton and twirled slower and slower on legs as limp as two wet noodles. Sometimes he slipped from his stilts, and when he turned a cartwheel he often sprawled like a clumsy bear cub.

The harder Taro tried, the more mistakes he made. Crowds no longer gathered to watch his clever tricks. Few threw copper coins into his hat, and none threw silver, and the day came when the monkey collected no money at all.

At bedtime that night, the musician and his wife talked things over.

"Poor fellow!" The husband shook his head. "Taro's growing old. He's getting weak. It's time for him to retire."

"Retire!" cried his wife. "Then what will we do with him?"

"I shall take him back where I found him," said the musician.

"Then what will we do without him?" the wife asked.

"I'm sure I can find a younger, stronger snow monkey," said her husband.

Taro's bed was outside on the porch, but through the paper *shoji* screen he could hear every word the man and woman said. He had to stuff a paw in his mouth to keep from calling out. None of his tricks, no matter how well he did them, could help him now. He needed advice from one wiser than he was.

Taro waited until the only sound from the other side of the screen was the wife's soft snoring. Then he crept from the porch, pushed open the gate, and ran down the path and into the forest. He ran until his weary legs would carry him no farther and collapsed beneath a large pine tree. When the snow monkey looked up, he saw that he was not alone.

A few feet away an enormous boar was digging up mushrooms by the light of the moon. The boar's snout was wrinkled, his belly sagged, his yellow tusks were chipped, and the hair on his hide bristled like pine needles. He stopped pawing long enough to glare at Taro with squinty little red eyes.

"Grumph!" the boar grunted. "What are you doing here?"

"Forgive me for disturbing you," Taro said. He bowed low, for a wild pig was known to be as short-tempered as he was sharp-witted. "I am in need of advice."

"You certainly are in need of something," said the boar, inspecting the skinny monkey. "You are a sorry sight."

"Soon I may look even sorrier!" said Taro. "My master the musician intends to take me back where I came from."

The boar snorted. "Returning to your own kind is nothing to be sorry about."

"It is for me. By now the musician is my own kind." Taro shivered. "And all I remember about the mountains is the cold."

"Then tell your master you want to stay," said the boar.

"I can't!" cried the monkey. "He doesn't understand a word I say! And even if he did, he thinks I am no longer useful."

"Hmmm," muttered the boar. "If you cannot tell him, you will have to show him instead." He closed his eyes in thought. "What does this musician like best?"

"Bokuden," Taro replied. "In all the world, he loves his son most."

"Then that's your answer." The old boar opened his eyes and winked at the monkey. "Go home and leave everything to me."

"To you? Don't I do something, too?" Taro asked.

"Of course," said the boar. "When you see me again, just give chase."

"Me?" squawked Taro. "Chase you?"

The boar grunted in reply and returned to digging mushrooms. The snow monkey dared not ask anything more. He stumbled back through the forest and down the path to the only home he knew.

◆　◆　◆　◆

The woman woke the monkey in the morning. "Watch Bokuden while I cook the breakfast rice," she told Taro. She put the baby down on the porch beside him.

The monkey stretched and then did a handstand. Bokuden grabbed Taro's stubby tail.

"*Eeek!*" squeaked the monkey.

Bokuden tugged harder. Taro teetered, lost his balance, and toppled over. Monkey and baby rolled together on the floor. Neither one saw the boar charge from the forest, rush up the path, and crash through the gate. But when the boar thundered onto the porch, Taro jumped up.

The bristles on the boar's back stood straight up, and his mouth was white with froth. He lowered his head and hooked one curved tusk through the sash of the Bokuden's kimono. Then the boar galloped off again with the baby bouncing from the sash like a puppet from a string.

Bokuden began to bawl. He howled louder than he'd ever howled in his life. His mother came running, but she was too late. She slid back the screen just in time to see the boar disappearing into the forest with her baby. "Stop! Stop!" she screamed, and ran to wake her husband.

The snow monkey stood on the porch and watched in disbelief, as if he were frozen. Then suddenly Taro remembered what the boar had told him. Finding a strength and speed he did not know he still had, the old monkey chased after the boar.

Waving his sword, the musician dashed from the house. His wife followed, weeping, at his heels. But Bokuden, the boar, and the monkey were nowhere to be seen.

"All is lost!" moaned the man in sorrow.

"Look!" the woman exclaimed suddenly. She pointed. "Look there!"

Taro was coming out of the woods. Slowly, he staggered up the path and through the broken gate. The snow monkey was bent over a bundle in his arms.

"He has Bokuden!" cried the musician. "My feeble old monkey has saved my baby from the boar!"

"Not so old he cannot run when he has to," his wife declared. She took Bokuden and hugged Taro. "Nor so feeble he cannot carry your son."

The musician wiped his eyes. "Never again will I doubt you," he said, bowing to the monkey. "Please honor us by remaining in our home."

The monkey bowed in return, slid open the screen, and stepped inside. The man brought him the softest cushion to sit upon, and the woman served him the biggest bowl of breakfast rice. When he had finished, the monkey jumped up and turned a perfect cartwheel.

Bokuden giggled, and the monkey laughed along with him.

THE STONE MONKEY

♦ A LEGEND FROM CHINA ♦

On a 2,000-year-old Chinese vase, there is a likeness of a golden monkey. Long ago, bands of golden langurs roamed the mountains of western China, but now they're found only in neighboring India. When the weather gets chilly, these rare monkeys hug each other for warmth.

A handsome golden langur, with its orange-yellow fur and turned-up nose, was probably the model for the monkey on the vase. And it may have been the model for the monkey king in this story, loved by Chinese children for many, many generations.

Once, in the western hills of China, a large egg lay in a nest in a tree on Flower-and-Fruit Mountain. The egg was too big to belong to a bird, even an ostrich, and the shell bulged oddly at one end. Not even Lord Buddha knew who or what might hatch from such a lopsided egg.

Early one morning, an earthquake struck Flower-and-Fruit Mountain. The ground shook, the tree swayed, and the egg came crashing down. The shell cracked open, and something strange tumbled out.

"Awk!" screeched an astonished bird. "It's a monkey!" He pecked at it cautiously. "A stone monkey!"

The bird flew off, eager to spread the news about a monkey made from rock. Although few believed him, a troop of curious monkeys climbed up Flower-and-Fruit Mountain to see   for themselves. Wide-eyed, they circled the creature lying on the ground beneath the tree.

"What good is a stone monkey?" asked one.

"It would make a good tombstone," another answered.

"It would make a good grindstone," said a third.

"It would be a nice statue," a fourth monkey suggested.

As the monkeys squabbled about which use best suited a stone monkey, it suddenly wiggled a toe.

"Tombstones don't move!" cried the monkeys.

The stone monkey sneezed.

The monkeys jumped back. "Grindstones can't sneeze!"

The stone monkey sat up and winked at the monkeys. "Can a statue wink?"

The monkeys scratched their heads, speechless.

"I do all those things," said the stone monkey, "and more besides." He stood and stretched. "As to what I'm good for, I am here to be your king."

"King!" whooped the excited monkeys. "What does a king do?"

"A king tells you what to do," said the stone monkey. "First, you must kneel before me. Like this." He touched his forehead to the ground. "Then follow me."

One by one, the band of monkeys knelt down and rubbed their noses on the ground. Then, single file, they marched down Flower-and-Fruit Mountain behind the stone monkey.

The delighted monkeys copied whatever their new king did and tried in every way to please him. When King Monkey called for royal dress, they wrapped him in golden robes as dazzling as the sun itself and gave him a sword studded with jewels. When he demanded the softest bed, the monkeys brought him four pillows stuffed with swans' down. Every day the monkey king's table was piled high with peaches and pomegranates. A hundred caged nightingales sang to him while he ate.

Still King Monkey was not satisfied. "Day in and day out, all I have to look at is monkey faces," he complained. "I want to see the world."

Lord Buddha shook his head. He had kept an eye and an ear on the monkey king ever since he'd hatched. Buddha listened but said nothing.

King Monkey ordered a sturdy raft to be built, with a sail the size of a cloud. He sailed it down the river to the sea and

across the ocean to a faraway land. There he was fortunate enough to meet a famous wizard.

"Master of Magic," said the stone monkey, "I am King of the Monkeys. Kindly tell me your secrets."

The wizard refused, but that did not discourage King Monkey. The stone monkey threw such terrible tantrums—and a number of other things besides—that the weary wizard agreed to share some of his secrets.

First he taught the monkey king to jump. All monkeys can jump, but with the wizard as his teacher, the stone monkey learned how to jump thousands of *li* in a single bound.

Next the wizard taught the monkey king to change shapes. The stone monkey learned how to transform himself into seventy-two different forms.

Last, although the monkey's mind was already overflowing with magic tricks, the wizard showed him how to fly. Humming loudly, the stone monkey flitted around the wizard's head like a mosquito.

"I am too clever to be just King Monkey," he exclaimed. "I shall be Lord of the Sky as well!"

The wizard shrugged, but when Lord Buddha heard the monkey's words, he whistled in exasperation.

"Ah!" said the stone monkey. "Feel the breeze! Now I can fly even faster!" With that, he stuck his snub nose in the air, flapped his arms, and flew up to Cloud Palace in the sky.

The palace was hidden behind dark storm clouds. "I am Lord of the Sky!" announced King Monkey. He clapped his hands. "Make rain!"

The clouds opened. Rain poured down until rivers spilled

over their banks and waterfalls rushed down the mountains. The stone monkey, busy jumping over the rainbow, paid no heed. "Look what I can do!" he crowed.

King Monkey waved the clouds away and ordered the sun to shine. It shone day and night, week after week. Trees and grasses dried, and the ocean shrank to a pond.

When King Monkey finally rolled the sun from the sky, those below stumbled about in the dark until he remembered to call out the moon.

Soon everyone on earth, from prince to plain people, was exasperated with the new Lord of the Sky. So the Dragon Prince paid a visit to the Buddha.

"Trouble everywhere!" Dragon Prince told Buddha. "And the monkey who calls himself king is to blame for it all."

"I shall speak to King Monkey," said Buddha. "I, too, have something to teach him."

The Buddha found the stone monkey strutting from cloud to cloud and boasting, "I am the cleverest in the universe!"

"What is it that you do, King Monkey?" asked Buddha.

"I can fly! I can change shape seventy-two times without stopping!" said the monkey. "And see how far I can jump!"

With one mighty leap, King Monkey soared over mountains and jungles, deserts and the seas. Moments later he bounded back. "Can you match that, Lord Buddha?" he asked.

"Let us make a bargain." Buddha smiled and held out his hand. "Stand here on my palm. If you can jump out of my hand, I agree that you deserve to be Lord of the Sky."

"Jump out of your hand?" The stone monkey laughed. "That's no contest at all."

"If you cannot," Buddha continued, "then you must return to earth and be a monkey, nothing more."

"Watch!" cried King Monkey.

The stone monkey hopped onto the Buddha's palm. Tucking his golden robe in his jeweled belt, he stood on tiptoe and gave a mighty jump. He sailed up and up, on and on, past the sun and the moon, the planets and the stars, until he saw nothing but empty space beyond. Here, beside the red pillars that hold up the heavens at the edge of the universe, King Monkey paused to catch his breath.

"I'll sign my name on a pillar," he said, "to show Lord Buddha how far I jumped."

The stone monkey bounded over the shortest pillar and unbuckled the sword from his belt. He raised the blade and suddenly realized he did not know how to write. He knew hundreds of tricks, but he could not even sign his name. All the stone monkey could do was carve a squiggle on the pillar with his sword.

"It looks like a monkey's tail!" cried King Monkey. "How very clever of me!"

Pleased with himself, the stone monkey hopped back into the Buddha's hand.

"Oh, there you are, King Monkey," said Buddha. "Are you ready to jump?"

"I am already finished!" sputtered the stone monkey. "I've jumped to the end of the universe and back. I can prove it!"

"How so?" asked Buddha.

"I carved my mark on one of the pillars that holds up the heavens."

"Does it look like this?" The Buddha opened his right hand and held up his fingers. On the little finger there was a tiny scratch shaped like a monkey's tail.

"It must be . . . ," King Monkey trembled. "Yes," he whispered.

Buddha turned his hand over and gently enclosed the stone monkey in his fingers. "The whole world lies within my grasp," he said. "When you jumped and thought you were out of sight, my hand was under you all the time."

King Monkey hung his head.

"No one, not even a magic monkey, can get beyond my reach or go beyond my sight. So keep our bargain, my boastful friend, and return to earth, where you belong."

The stone monkey went back to Flower-and-Fruit Mountain. He was no longer Lord of the Sky. He wasn't even King of the Monkeys anymore. He returned to the tree where he'd hatched from the big stone egg and became an ordinary monkey.

◆ ◆ ◆ ◆ ◆ ◆ ◆ ◆ ◆ ◆ ◆ ◆ ◆ ◆ ◆ ◆ ◆ ◆ ◆ ◆

Slowly, slowly,
Catches the monkey.
MEANING: Do not hurry a difficult task.
—*Proverb, Hong Kong*

◆ ◆ ◆ ◆ ◆ ◆ ◆ ◆ ◆ ◆ ◆ ◆ ◆ ◆ ◆ ◆ ◆ ◆ ◆ ◆

Uncle Monkey and the Ghosts

♦ A FILIPINO FOLKTALE ♦

Wild monkeys still live in the forests on some of the Philippine Islands. The monkey in this story is probably a pig-tailed macaque. It gets its name from the short, almost hairless tail that curls over its back just like a piglet's.

The carabao is the Philippine water buffalo. Because the chevrotain resembles a tiny deer, it's commonly called a mouse deer.

Uncle Monkey was the wisest animal in the forest. All the others, from the little *butiki* lizard to the big carabao, came to him for advice. The monkey's perch was in a breadfruit tree where he could keep a watchful eye on everyone and everything.

Not far from the breadfruit tree stood a bamboo hut on stilts. It was the home of Jojo the Hunter. All the forest creatures, except for Uncle Monkey, were afraid of him. Whenever the hunter came near, they ran away as fast as they could. That suited Jojo, for he preferred his own pets.

His favorites were his dog, his cat, his rooster, his parrot, and his sturdy Philippine pony. Over the years, as Jojo grew old, his animals grew old along with him, and when the white-haired hunter died, his aged pets lay down and died, too. Only the parrot was left, and it flew away.

People from the *barangay*, the village beyond the forest, buried the hunter and his pets together. Then they carved these words on a stone:

HERE LIES JOJO,
THE MIGHTY HUNTER.
WITH HIM ARE BURIED
AYSO, HIS DOG,
BYSO, HIS PONY,
POOSO, HIS CAT,
AND MAYNOOK, HIS ROOSTER.
MAY THEY REST IN PEACE.

Now the wild forest animals could be at peace, too.

The boar could sleep in the shade beneath the hut on stilts, for Jojo no longer hunted him with a spear.

The carabao could wallow all day in the rice field, for he no longer feared being snared by Jojo on his pony.

The mouse deer could nibble the radishes in the garden, as there was no dog to chase her away.

The rat could nest snugly in the hut's thatched roof, as there was no cat to catch him.

Even the locust could sing as loudly as he wished without fearing that the rooster might snap him up in midsong. And they could all nap without Loro the parrot disturbing them, for Jojo's noisy parrot had disappeared.

Early one morning, someone—or something—spoiled their happiness. The boar was the first to run to Uncle Monkey in the breadfruit tree.

"Help!" cried the boar. Every bristle on his back stood straight up in terror.

"What happened?" asked Uncle Monkey. "Did you see a ghost?"

"YES!" squealed the boar. "Jojo is back!"

"Jojo?" The monkey stared at the boar. "That cannot be."

"I heard his loud voice!" the boar cried. "It woke me up!"

"You were dreaming," Uncle Monkey told him, "and you heard yourself snoring."

"It was Jojo the Hunter." The boar quivered from snout to tail. "I even felt the sting of his spear!"

"You most likely felt a tick," said Uncle Monkey. "Stop worrying and finish your nap under those bamboo trees."

"But what about Jojo?" asked the boar.

"I'll watch out for the hunter," Uncle Monkey promised, "or his ghost."

Before long, Uncle Monkey saw the carabao lumbering toward the breadfruit tree.

"UNCLE MONKEY!" bellowed the water buffalo.

The monkey put his paws over his ears. "What's wrong?"

"Everything!" groaned the carabao. "First I heard Jojo's pony neigh! When I tried to run, I got caught in a snare! And now I feel Jojo's arrows sticking in my sides!"

"You heard an owl hoot," Uncle Monkey comforted him.

"You tangled your feet in a vine. And the prickles you feel are the bites of blowflies. Brush off the flies with your tail and join your friend the boar in the bamboo grove."

"But what about Jojo's pony?" asked the water buffalo.

"I'll watch for Byso—or Byso's ghost," promised Uncle Monkey.

Uncle Monkey didn't see the ghost of Jojo or his pony, but he did see the mouse deer slipping out from the forest shadows.

"Good morning!" he called to her.

"*Sssssh!*" whispered the mouse deer. "Jojo's dog is back!"

"How do you know?" Uncle Monkey asked.

"I heard Ayso barking!" The mouse deer trembled. "He came so close I could feel his whiskers!"

"What you heard was a tree frog croaking," Uncle Monkey told the mouse deer. "And what you felt was a burr caught in your tail. It's still there."

The mouse deer twirled around, trying to shake off the burr.

"The boar and the carabao will keep you company in the bamboo grove while I watch for Ayso—or Ayso's ghost," said Uncle Monkey.

The monkey looked from left to right, up and down, and over his shoulder, but he did not see a dog. What he saw was the rat dashing to his breadfruit tree.

"A fine day, Brother Rat!" Uncle Monkey called.

"A terrible day!" squeaked the rat. "The cat's come back!"

"Come back? Are you quite certain?"

"Quite!" cried the rat. "Just before sunup, I heard Pooso meow. I saw his yellow eyes gleaming in the dark like moons!"

"Your ears are playing tricks," Uncle Monkey told him, "and you can't believe your eyes. You heard a night bird calling and saw two glowworms shining."

The rat twitched his nose and sniffed. "If you say so. . . ."

"Hide in the bamboo with the boar and the buffalo and the mouse deer. If I see Pooso—or Pooso's ghost—I'll warn you," promised Uncle Monkey.

Scarcely had the rat scuttled into the bamboo before Uncle Monkey had another visitor.

"Help! Help! Help!" chirped the locust, flying in circles around the breadfruit tree. "Maynook the rooster is after me!"

"I don't see him," said Uncle Monkey.

"I heard him cock-a-doodle-doo! He's going to eat me!"

"That wasn't Maynook crowing." Uncle Monkey shook his head. "It was the cry of a noisy gecko. Fly to the bamboo grove. The boar, the buffalo, the mouse deer, and the rat are already there, waiting."

"Waiting for what, Uncle Monkey?" asked the locust.

"Waiting for me to go on a ghost hunt," said Uncle Monkey, jumping down from the breadfruit tree.

Although Uncle Monkey had never seen a ghost, he couldn't say for certain that there weren't any. But he would not admit such a thing, not even to himself. He hopped jauntily down the path to Jojo's house, his skinny tail bouncing above his back like a curl of ribbon.

Cautiously Uncle Monkey pushed open Jojo's door and looked about. Except for a few cobwebs, everything was just as the hunter had left it. He listened but heard no strange noises. A frightened spider skittered across the floor without a sound.

"Is anyone here?" Uncle Monkey called.

"Ho! Ho! Ho!"

The booming laugh rattled the hut and sent shivers dancing along Uncle Monkey's backbone. His tail uncurled, and every hair on his head stood up. The laugh sounded just like the old hunter's.

"Is—is that you, Jojo?" he asked.

A dog barked, and then a cat yowled.

"Ayso?" Uncle Monkey whirled around. "Pooso?"

A rooster crowed. A horse whinnied.

"Maynook? Byso?" shouted Uncle Monkey. "Where are you?"

Something swooped down from the rafters and flapped wildly around the hut. "Here!"

Uncle Monkey ducked. "Loro!" he cried. "Jojo's parrot! And you're his rooster as well. And his cat! And his dog! And his horse! You even pretended to be old Jojo himself! Shame on you, you tricky old bird!" scolded Uncle Monkey.

"Smart bird! Smart bird!" Loro cackled. "I can even fool wise Uncle Monkey!"

"Then you're too smart to stay where you're not wanted!" declared Uncle Monkey. He snatched a broom from its hook and chased the parrot around the room.

"Ho! Ho! Ho!" laughed Loro again, and flapped toward the door. But he could not get out. The water buffalo, the boar, the mouse deer, the rat, and the locust blocked the doorway.

Uncle Monkey waved his broom. "Here's your ghost," he told them. "One parrot with five voices."

With a flash of red and blue and green feathers, Loro skimmed over their heads and flew out the door.

"Can't catch me!" the parrot squawked.

To Loro's disappointment no one even tried to catch him. The carabao went back to wallowing in his rice paddy. The boar dozed once more beneath Jojo's hut. The rat returned to the rooftop, the locust sang outside the door, and the mouse deer browsed in the garden. Everything was quiet until, deep in the forest, a horse neighed, a dog barked, a cat meowed, and a rooster crowed. But those noises no longer frightened the animals. They knew that Loro the parrot was up to his tricks again.

Then they heard a different sound. Someone was laughing, but it wasn't Jojo's ghost. It wasn't Jojo's parrot, either. This time it was Uncle Monkey, sitting in his breadfruit tree, chuckling to himself.

❖ ❖

The fruit that tastes sweet in a monkey's mouth
may turn sour in its stomach.
MEANING: What seems good today may be bad tomorrow.
—*Proverb, India*

❖ ❖

Prince Rama and the Monkey Chieftain

◆ FROM THE RAMAYANA, AN EPIC POEM FROM INDIA ◆

In India, the big, long-tailed gray langur monkeys are known as hanuman monkeys. They are the namesakes of Hanuman, the heroic monkey chieftain who once helped humankind. For this reason, hanuman monkeys are protected in India today and permitted to roam freely about the countryside.

In ancient times, poets told of a prince named Rama who once ruled in the land of India. Since he was both wise and generous, everyone in his kingdom, from the lowly to the highborn, was content. Rama was wed to a beautiful princess named Sita. He prized his gentle-hearted wife above all else on earth.

Prince Rama was an able hunter and a skilled archer. One morning, he tracked a large stag deep into the forest, hoping to make a soft rug for Sita from its hide. When Rama returned from his hunt, he found the palace in an uproar.

The wooden lattice on Sita's window hung in splinters, Sita's couch was overturned, and Sita's jewels were scattered on the floor like shells on the sand. Sita herself was missing.

"Search the palace!" Rama ordered. "The princess cannot vanish!"

Suddenly the prince had a fearful thought. "Perhaps she followed me on the hunt! Perhaps some wild animal . . . "

He ran from the palace and into the forest, calling "Sita!" over and over again. His only answer came from a band of monkeys in the trees. Rama hesitated, listening to their chatter, for in that time man and beast understood each other's speech.

"Our warrior chief has knowledge of the princess," one monkey called. "If you would hear, then come with us."

Eagerly Prince Rama followed the monkeys. They pushed through tangled undergrowth and beneath palms so thick with fronds that Rama could not see the sky. At last they came to a large clearing. In the middle, under a bower of bright flowers, sat a huge gray monkey on a cushioned throne. Smaller monkeys surrounded him, waving away mosquitoes with palm-leaf fans.

The big monkey rose to his feet. "I am Hanuman the Monkey Chief."

"And I am Prince Rama. I seek word of the Princess Sita."

"Then I must give you bad news." Hanuman placed a hairy paw on Rama's shoulder. "The princess has been stolen."

"Stolen?" cried Rama.

"With my own eyes, I saw the princess hurtling through the sky in a chariot drawn by jackals," replied the monkey chief. "With my own ears, I heard her screams."

"That could not be!" Rama insisted. "You've mistaken another for my Sita."

"She dropped this as a sign." The monkey chief put a jeweled hair ornament in the prince's hand.

The prince gazed at it. "Sita wore this when we wed."

"The chariot turned to the south, toward the island of Lanka. Only one dares to go there." Hanuman scowled. "Ravana."

"The Lord of Death!" cried Rama. "If he has taken Sita, my gentle wife is lost. I cannot match Ravana's power."

"Nor can I," said Hanuman. "But the two of us might."

Puzzled, the prince stared at the monkey. "Why should you want to put yourself in danger?"

"Helping you helps us all. If we destroy Ravana, we can put an end to evil."

"And we can rescue Sita!" Rama said joyfully.

Within a week, ten hundred of Rama's foot soldiers and ten thousand of Hanuman's monkeys had gathered. Joining forces, the two armies stretched out across the green land like a dark shadow. They marched toward India's southern shore, but their progress was slow. The monsoon season had begun, and day after day rain poured from the sky. Shallow streams became boiling rivers, and jungle paths were soups of mud. Soldiers stumbled over banyan roots as thick as elephant trunks, and vines twisted about their ankles like pythons. The monkeys' hands bled from swinging through thorn trees, and everyone feared the hungry tigers that prowled the jungle.

At last, the two rain-soaked armies reached the Indian Ocean. Far offshore, on the island of Lanka, they saw a white marble palace rising from the mist like a mirage.

"There!" Prince Rama shouted, pointing. "The demon Ravana holds Sita prisoner within those tower walls."

"How can we get there?" one soldier asked. "The channel is too wide to swim, and we have no boats."

Rama groaned and shook his head. He had thought only of reaching India's southern shore. Now that he was here, almost close enough to Sita to smell her perfume, the long journey seemed in vain.

"I have an idea," said Hanuman.

Rama turned to the monkey chief with hope. "What?"

"We will make a road across the water," Hanuman explained.

"A bridge?" asked Rama doubtfully. "Our time is too short, and the water is too deep."

"Not for my monkeys," Hanuman replied.

At his command, ten thousand monkeys went to work. Some scattered to the trees and began tearing off branches. Others gathered piles of stones and mountains of rocks. Whatever a monkey could cut or dig, lift, and carry, he threw into the sea. In only five days' time, a rough road stretched across the water that separated the mainland from the island. As soon as the final rock was pushed into place, the soldiers and monkey warriors rushed across the bridge to storm Ravana's fortress.

Ravana's demons were waiting. Monsters of every description fought Prince Rama's armies. Some were snarling beasts with the heads of tigers and the bodies of crocodiles. One was a sky-scraping giant, big enough to swallow a monkey whole. Others were mean, stinging little imps, no larger than wasps. A few were so small that neither man nor monkey knew they were about until they felt the bites of their weapons. Whatever their shape or size, all of Ravana's soldiers were armed with swords or spears, with bows and arrows, or with pikes and pitchforks. They darted

about like lightning bolts flung by Indra, the God of Thunder.

When the fighting ended, thousands of demons had been destroyed, but an equal number of Rama's men and Hanuman's monkeys lay dead or dying on the battlefield.

"We fought bravely to the end," the weary prince declared.

"Perhaps the end has not yet come," said the monkey chief.

Hanuman summoned all his strength and gave a mighty leap. Parting the clouds, he soared high into the air. When his toes touched ground again, he was in India's Himalaya mountains.

On the highest slopes, surrounded by snowy fields, grew herbs with magic healing powers. The monkey chief gathered armloads of them, pulling the plants so frantically that he tore off a mountaintop in his haste. Then, bent beneath his bundles, the monkey chief headed back to Lanka. The tingling smell of herbs drifted on the wind and began to work its magic on the injured even before Hanuman landed. He walked among them, sprinkling men and monkeys with herbs. Wounds healed, bones mended, and the dead woke up as if from sleep.

From his palace towers, Ravana watched his enemies revive. Grasping a sword in each of his dozen arms, he jumped into his war chariot, drawn by four vultures, and flew over the battlefield. Those below cried out in terror, for the Lord of Death was horrible to see.

Sprouting from Ravana's shoulders were ten necks that

held up ten huge heads. Each head had bulging eyes that rolled about in opposite directions so that nothing escaped Ravana's notice. A bone-chilling war cry came from each of his mouths.

"Stand back!" Prince Rama ordered his warriors. "This monster is mine! Only I can avenge Sita."

The vultures swooped down to the ground, and the war chariot stopped so suddenly that sparks flew from beneath its iron wheels. Shrieking, Ravana sprang out and attacked Rama with his swords.

The prince struck back, but Ravana's skin was as hard as marble. Rama's spear could not pierce it, and his sword bent against it. Whenever the prince came close, Ravana laughed and changed shape. Sometimes he became a howling jackal or a snarling tiger with teeth like daggers. At other times, he was invisible. Once, when Rama was about to deliver a crushing blow with his battle-ax, he thought he saw the beautiful Sita kneeling before him. The prince held back until he realized that her long black braid had become a writhing serpent. This was not his wife. It was another of Ravana's wicked tricks.

Stumbling with exhaustion, Rama reached in his quiver for an arrow. Only one remained. He fit the last arrow to his bow and stretched the string back farther than he ever had before. When he released it, the brass-tipped arrow sprang forward with such force that the earth shook. A cloud of dust rose up, covering the sun, and they all dropped to their knees, except for one. The prince's arrow had pierced Ravana's cruel heart.

Rama looked down at the motionless figure sprawled before him. Then, taking one of Ravana's own swords, he cut off each of the demon's ten heads.

"Now it is truly ended," a weary Prince Rama said. He turned to Hanuman and bowed. "I am in your debt."

"Friends help one another," answered the monkey chief, bowing in return. Then he led his battle-worn monkeys back across the bridge they had built and along the tangled jungle paths to their home in India.

Rama lost no time in freeing Sita from her prison on Lanka. They flew back to their own palace in a golden chariot drawn by wild swans, and, throughout the rest of Prince Rama's long reign, Princess Sita remained by his side.

◆ Monkey Trivia ◆

What is a monkey?

You're right if you said a primate. Zoologists put monkeys and apes in the order of Primates—spelled with a capital *P*. But even the experts aren't sure why a monkey is called a monkey.

Perhaps our English word *monkey* came from an epic animal tale told in Germany about 600 years ago. In the story "Reynard the Fox," the son of Martin the Ape was known as Moneke. Said aloud, his name sounds a lot like monkey.

Where do monkeys live today?

Monkeys live in tropical areas of ninety-two countries.

How do New World monkeys differ from Old World monkeys?

All the monkeys in Central and South America live in trees, so they're smaller than their Old World cousins. They're noisier, too, because on their treetop perches they're safer from enemies.

Some monkeys in Africa and Asia live in trees. Others, like baboons, are ground dwellers and only climb trees for protection.

Old World monkeys, except the colobus, have thumbs like humans have. In the New World, only a capuchin has a working thumb.

All New World monkeys have tails, and many can use them for grasping. Some Old World monkeys have tails, some don't, and none can swing by them.

The nostrils in the nose of a New World monkey are far apart. An Old World monkey has nostrils close together (like ours).

How big is a monkey?

Largest of the monkeys is the mandrill of Africa. This sturdy ground monkey can weigh 100 pounds.

Smallest is the South American pygmy marmoset. Weighing only a couple of ounces, it's tiny enough to put in your pocket. Two centuries ago, a stylish European lady might attach a live marmoset monkey to her hat as a decoration.

Are monkeys left- or right-handed?

Most animals—both you and your dog, for example—favor one hand or paw over the other. Monkeys are equally handy with either.

How does a monkey talk?

Monkeys use gestures and facial expressions to communicate, just as we do. And, depending on its mood, a monkey may yelp, click, grunt, growl, screech, sing, cough, howl, squawk, scream, whoop, whistle, chatter, groan, croak, or sigh. The small squirrel monkey purrs like a kitten when it eats, and a spider monkey barks like a terrier when it sees danger.

Aren't most monkeys brown?

Some are, but certainly not all of them. The Japanese macaque is brown, but it has a bright red face. Monkeys come in as many colors as a paint box, and some change color as they grow. The proboscis monkey of Borneo has a long dangling nose that looks like an orange banana. It's born with a deep blue face that turns pink when it's an adult. Howler monkeys come in candy colors of licorice, chocolate, butterscotch, orange, cherry, and lemon.

How lucky that all monkeys see everything in full color!

Do any monkeys stay up at night?

A douroucouli, or owl monkey of South America, is the world's only night-active monkey. All other monkeys sleep at night and, like the rest of us, look around for breakfast the first thing in the morning.

What do monkeys eat?

Most monkeys are vegetarians and live on greens and fruits. But that doesn't mean they don't enjoy special treats, like a few termites, an occasional lizard, or your bag of peanuts.

Monkeys, wherever in the world they live, are endangered by habitat loss. What happens to them tomorrow is up to all of us today.

Bibliography

• •

MONKEYS IN AFRICA AND MADAGASCAR

Why a Monkey's Not a Man

Benin was once known as the Kingdom of Dahomey. When the French overthrew the Oba, or king, the empire became part of Nigeria in French West Africa. A half century later, Dahomey declared independence, changed its name to Benin, and established a republic. Although French remains the language of literature, this old story comes from oral tradition. It's based on a fable told in the dialect of Ewe by the Fon, a native people.

The People of the Trees

Black-and-white Colobus monkeys were once abundant in the Congo, where this "how come" story originated. Now, like many other African animals, these handsome monkeys are endangered. Sharing stories about them may help to secure their future.

The story was adapted from "The Scrawny Old Man and the Scrawny Old Woman" in *Folk Tales of All Nations*, F. H. Lee, editor (Tudor Publishing Company, New York, 1930).

The Monkey, the Rats, the Cheese

Like many fables, this cautionary folktale uses animals to illustrate the message. In this case, two not-so-bright rats and a much-too-clever monkey reflect not animal behavior but human nature. The maxim they deliver: If two would share something equally, let one do the dividing and the other have the first choice.

The story was adapted from "Dividing the Cheese" in *Folk Tales of All Nations*, F. H. Lee, editor (Tudor Publishing Company, New York, 1930).

THE BABOON AND THE SHARK

Although storytelling was an important part of village life in Liberia, tribal literature was not written down until the beginning of the twentieth century. This tale of a quick-witted monkey who used his head to save his heart was told for many years before it ever saw print. A similar version in Japan is titled "The Jellyfish and the Monkey," while a Chinese story tells about a monkey who outsmarts a crocodile to hold on to his heart.

Adapted from "Shark and Monkey" in *Liberian Folklore: A Compilation of Ninety-Nine Folktales with Some Proverbs* by A. Doris Banks Henries (Macmillan and Company, London, 1966).

MONKEY ANCESTORS

No monkey book would be complete without looking at lemurs, for they're a connecting link between yesterday's prehistoric primates and today's monkeys. Because of their antics and their sometimes scary appearance, stories and superstitions have grown up around them.

My primary source for lemur facts and fancies was *Primates: The Amazing World of Lemurs, Monkeys, and Apes* by Barbara Sleeper, photography by Art Wolfe (Chronicle Books, San Francisco, 1997).

MONKEYS IN THE AMERICAS

The First Monkeys

The Mayans were the first South American people to record both their political history and their mythology. One of the few books to survive the centuries is the *Popol Vuh*, which means "the collection of written leaves." This pre-Columbian work was lost for a long time and only rediscovered 150 years ago. The *Popol Vuh* is the source for this Mayan creation myth.

Many editions of the book are available, for example *Popol Vuh: The Definitive Edition of the Mayan Book of the Dawn of Life and the Glories of Gods and Kings, Dennis Tedlock*, translator (Simon and Schuster, New York, 1996).

The Spider Monkey's Close Shave

This story is excerpted from "The Tale of a Tortoise and of a Mischievous Monkey" in *The Brown Fairy Book* by Andrew Lang (Dover Publications, New York, 1990 reprint of the 1904 edition). Lang's lengthy folktale is also the basis for Anne Rockwell's picture book *The Monkey's Whiskers* (Parents' Magazine Press, New York, 1971). Although Lang cited a story from *Folk-lore Brésilien* by Frederico José de Santa-Anna Nery (Perrin, Paris, 1889) as his source, Ms. Rockwell points out that the European style of the tale suggests that its origin may have been Portugal.

I chose the agile spider monkey as the story's lead character because the Aztec people associated it with song, dance, and pleasure. Those qualities best suit the monkey in the folktale.

So Say the Little Monkeys

Often a story inspires a saying, but in this instance the proverb came first. In their collection of stories from South America, M. A. Jagendorf and R. S. Boggs offer a tale that explains how the happy-go-lucky behavior of small squirrel monkeys gave rise to the popular saying "So say the little monkeys." The theme is not unlike Aesop's "The Ant and the Grasshopper."

Adapted from *The King of the Mountains: A Treasury of Latin American Folk Tales* by M. A. Jagendorf and R. S. Boggs (Vanguard Press, Inc., New York, 1960).

Tasi and the Oranges

As with "The Spider Monkey's Close Shave," this story was also taken from "The Tale of a Tortoise and of a Mischievous Monkey" in *The Brown Fairy Book* by Andrew Lang (Dover Publications, New York, 1990 reprint of the 1904 edition).

In retelling the story, Lang followed the style of his time and didn't attempt to identify the sex or species of monkey or to pinpoint the story's location. Reasoning that today's readers want to know more, I chose a howler monkey—Brazil's morning alarm clock—as my main character. A big, noisy, red-furred female howler such as Tasi seemed a fair match for the farmer.

MONKEYS IN ASIA

The Monkey Keeper

This parable from China is from *Chinese Fairy Tales and Fantasies*, translated and edited by Moss Roberts with the assistance of C. N. Tay (Pantheon Books, New York, 1979).

THE SNOW MONKEY AND THE BOAR

This fairy tale was adapted from "The Sagacious Monkey and the Boar" from *The Japanese Fairy Book* by Yei Theodora Ozaka (Dover Publications, New York, 1967). "The Sagacious Monkey and the Boar" was a favorite of the *hanashika*, the Japanese storyteller. Traditionally, a fairy tale depends on a supernatural happening to catch a listener's ear. In this more realistic "fairy story," the *hanashika* simply wants the audience to be sympathetic to an appealing monkey.

THE STONE MONKEY

In China, literary references to a monkey king date back a thousand years. Classic among them is "The Stone Monkey," in which Lord Buddha gently teaches the cocky monkey king a lesson. The many variations of this story differ mainly in the details. The *li* mentioned in this retelling is a measurement of distance, about half a kilometer.

I based my version of this story on "The King of the Monkeys" from the book *Tales of a Chinese Grandmother* by Frances Carpenter (Charles E. Tuttle Co., Boston/Tokyo, 2002). I also consulted "The Monkey Who Would Be King" from *Myths and Legends* by Anthony Horowitz (Kingfisher Books, New York, 1994).

UNCLE MONKEY AND THE GHOSTS

The story was adapted from "Mr. Monk and the Frightened Animals" from the book *Folk Tales from the Far East*, by Charles H. Meeker (John C. Winston Company, Chicago, 1927).

While this tale is based on Filipino lore, and the animals

are native to southeast Asia, the storytelling style shows strong Spanish and American influences from the past century.

In the Philippines, you don't have to be a relative to be called uncle, or *tito*. An older man who's admired is often referred to that way, especially by children, as a sign of respect.

PRINCE RAMA AND THE MONKEY CHIEFTAIN

"Prince Rama and the Monkey Chieftain" is from the *Ramayana*, an epic poem first written down in Sanskrit about 1000 B.C. Each autumn, the story of Rama and Sita and Hanuman is acted out in celebrations across India.

This version is based on "The Tale of the Monkey God" in *Magical Beasts* (The Enchanted World Series by the editors of Time/Life Books (Alexandria, VA, 1985).